THE UNPLEASANTNESS AT THE BELLONA CLUB

MYSTERIES BY DOROTHY L. SAYERS

THE UNPLEASANTNESS AT THE BELLONA CLUB

A Lord Peter Wimsey Mystery

DOROTHY L. SAYERS

HARPER

NEW YORK • LONDON • TORONTO • SYDNEY

A hardcover edition of this book was published in 1928 by Harper
& Row Publishers, Inc. It is reprinted here by arrangement with
the Estate of Anthony Fleming.

THE UNPLEASANTNESS AT THE BELLONA CLUB. Copyright © 1928 by
Dorothy Leigh Sayers Fleming. Copyright renewed © 1956
by Dorothy Leigh Sayers Fleming. Afterword copyright © 2013 by
John Curran. All rights reserved. Printed in the United States
of America. No part of this book may be used or reproduced in
any manner whatsoever without written permission except in the
case of brief quotations embodied in critical articles and reviews.
For information, address HarperCollins Publishers, 195 Broadway,
New York, NY 10007.

HarperCollins books may be purchased for educational, business,
or sales promotional use. For information, please e-mail the
Special Markets Department at SPsales@harpercollins.com.

First Harper Perennial edition published 1987. Reissued in 1993.
First Bourbon Street Books edition published 2014.

Library of Congress Cataloging-in-Publication Data is available
upon request.

ISBN 978-0-06-231191-7

19 20 21 22 DIX/LSC 10 9 8 7 6 5 4

WIMSEY, Peter Death Bredon, D.S.O.; *born* 1890, *2nd son of* Mortimer Gerald Bredon Wimsey, 15th Duke of Denver, and of Honoria Lucasta, *daughter of* Francis Delagardie of Bellingham Manor, Hants.

Educated: Eton College and Balliol College, Oxford (1st class honours, Sch. of Mod. Hist. 1912); served with H. M. Forces 1914/18 (Major, Rifle Brigade). *Author of:* "Notes on the Collecting of Incunabula," "The Murderer's Vade-Mecum," etc. *Recreations:* Criminology; bibliophily; music; cricket.

Clubs: Marlborough; Egotists'. *Residences:* 110A Piccadilly, W.; Bredon Hall, Duke's Denver, Norfolk.

Arms: Sable, 3 mice courant, argent; crest, a domestic cat couched as to spring, proper; motto: As my Whimsy takes me.

CONTENTS

CONTENTS

I

Old Mossy-Face

"What in the world, Wimsey, are you doing in this Morgue?" demanded Captain Fentiman, flinging aside the "Evening Banner" with the air of a man released from an irksome duty.

"Oh, I wouldn't call it that," retorted Wimsey, amiably. "Funeral Parlor at the very least. Look at the marble. Look at the furnishings. Look at the palms and the chaste bronze nude in the corner."

"Yes, and look at the corpses. Place always reminds me of that old thing in 'Punch,' you know—'Waiter, take away Lord Whatsisname, he's been dead two days.' Look at Old Ormsby there, snoring like a hippopotamus. Look at my revered grandpa—dodders in here at ten every morning, collects the

'Morning Post' and the armchair by the fire, and becomes part of the furniture till the evening. Poor old devil. Suppose I'll be like that one of these days. I wish to God Jerry had put me out with the rest of 'em. What's the good of coming through for this sort of thing? What'll you have?"

"Dry martini," said Wimsey. "And you? Two dry martinis, Fred, please. Cheer up. All this remembrance-day business gets on your nerves, don't it? It's my belief most of us would be only too pleased to chuck these community hysterics if the beastly newspapers didn't run it for all it's worth. However, it don't do to say so. They'd hoof me out of the Club if I raised my voice beyond a whisper."

"They'd do that anyway, whatever you were saying," said Fentiman, gloomily. "What *are* you doing here?"

"Waitin' for Colonel Marchbanks," said Wimsey. "Bung-ho!"

"Dining with him?"

"Yes."

Fentiman nodded quietly. He knew that young Marchbanks had been killed at Hill 60, and that the Colonel was wont to give a small, informal dinner on Armistice night to his son's intimate friends.

"I don't mind old Marchbanks," he said, after a pause. "He's a dear old boy."

Wimsey assented.

"And how are things going with you?" he asked.

"Oh, rotten as usual. Tummy all wrong and no money. What's the damn good of it, Wimsey? A man goes and fights for his country, gets his inside gassed out, and loses his job, and all they give him is the privilege of marching past the Cenotaph once a year and paying four shillings in the pound income-tax. Sheila's queer too—overwork, poor girl. It's pretty damnable for a man to have to live on his wife's earnings, isn't it? I can't help it, Wimsey. I go sick and have to chuck jobs up. Money—I never thought of money before the War, but I swear nowadays I'd commit any damned crime to get hold of a decent income."

Fentiman's voice had risen in nervous excitement. A shocked veteran, till then invisible in a neighboring armchair, poked out a lean head like a tortoise and said "Sh!" viperishly.

"Oh, I wouldn't do that," said Wimsey, lightly. "Crime's a skilled occupation, y' know. Even a comparative imbecile like myself can play the giddy sleuth on the amateur Moriarty. If you're thinkin' of puttin' on a false mustache and lammin' a millionaire on the head, don't do it. That disgustin' habit you have of smoking cigarettes down to the last millimeter would betray you anywhere. I'd only have to come on with a magnifyin' glass and a pair of callipers to say 'The criminal is my dear old friend George Fentiman. Arrest that man!' You might not think it, but I am ready to sacrifice my nearest and dearest in order to curry favor with the police and get a par. in the papers."

Fentiman laughed, and ground out the offending cigarette stub on the nearest ash-tray.

"I wonder anybody cares to know you," he said. The strain and bitterness had left his voice and he sounded merely amused.

"They wouldn't," said Wimsey, "only they think I'm too well-off to have any brains. It's like hearing that the Earl of Somewhere is taking a leading part in a play. Everybody takes it for granted he must act rottenly. I'll tell you my secret. All my criminological investigations are done for me by a 'ghost' at £3 a week, while I get the headlines and frivol with well-known journalists at the Savoy."

"I find you refreshing, Wimsey," said Fentiman, languidly. "You're not in the least witty, but you have a kind of obvious facetiousness which reminds me of the less exacting class of music-hall."

"It's the self-defense of the first-class mind against the superior person," said Wimsey. "But, look here, I'm sorry to hear about Sheila. I don't want to be offensive, old man, but why don't you let me—"

"Damned good of you," said Fentiman, "but I don't care to. There's honestly not the faintest chance I could ever pay you, and I haven't quite got to the point yet—"

"Here's Colonel Marchbanks," broke in Wimsey, "we'll talk about it another time. Good evening, Colonel."

"Evening, Peter. Evening, Fentiman. Beautiful day it's been. No—no cocktails, thanks, I'll stick to whisky. So sorry to keep you waiting like this, but I was having a yarn with poor old Grainger upstairs. He's in a baddish way, I'm afraid. Between you and me, Penberthy doesn't think he'll last out the winter. Very sound man, Penberthy—wonderful, really, that he's kept the old man going so long with his lungs in that frail state. Ah, well! it's what we must all come to. Dear me, there's your grand-father, Fentiman. He's another of Penberthy's miracles. He must be ninety, if he's a day. Will you excuse me for a moment? I must just go and speak to him."

Wimsey's eyes followed the alert, elderly figure as it crossed the spacious smoking room, pausing now and again to exchange greetings with a fellow-member of the Bellona Club. Drawn close to the huge fireplace stood a great chair with ears after the Victorian pattern. A pair of spindle shanks with neatly-buttoned shoes propped on a footstool were all that was visible of General Fentiman.

"Queer, isn't it," muttered his grandson, "to think that for Old Mossy-face there the Crimea is still *the* War, and the Boer business found him too old to go out. He was given his commis-sion at seventeen, you know—was wounded at Majuba—"

He broke off. Wimsey was not paying attention. He was still watching Colonel Marchbanks.

The Colonel came back to them, walking very quietly and precisely. Wimsey rose and went to meet him.

"I say, Peter," said the Colonel, his kind face gravely troubled, "just come over here a moment. I'm afraid something rather unpleasant has happened."

Fentiman looked round, and something in their manner made him get up and follow them over to the fire.

Wimsey bent down over General Fentiman and drew the "Morning Post" gently away from the gnarled old hands, which lay clasped over the thin chest. He touched the shoulder—put his hand under the white head huddled against the side of the chair. The Colonel watched him anxiously. Then, with a quick jerk, Wimsey lifted the quiet figure. It came up all of a piece, stiff as a wooden doll.

Fentiman laughed. Peal after hysterical peal shook his throat. All round the room, scandalized Bellonians creaked to their gouty feet, shocked by the unmannerly noise.

"Take him away!" said Fentiman, "take him away. He's been dead two days! So are you! So am I! We're all dead and we never noticed it!"

II

The Queen Is Out

It is doubtful which occurrence was more disagreeable to the
senior members of the Bellona Club—the grotesque death of
General Fentiman in their midst or the indecent neurasthenia
of his grandson. Only the younger men felt no sense of outrage;
they knew too much. Dick Challoner—known to his intimates as
Tin-Tummy Challoner, owing to the fact that he had been fitted
with a spare part after the second battle of the Somme—took the
gasping Fentiman away into the deserted library for a stiffener.
The Club Secretary hurried in, in his dress-shirt and trousers,
the half-dried lather still clinging to his jaws. After one glance
he sent an agitated waiter to see if Dr. Penberthy was still in
the Club. Colonel Marchbanks laid a large silk handkerchief
reverently over the rigid face in the armchair and remained
quietly standing. A little circle formed about the edge of the